THE BOY BEHIND THE BLOG

KARTIK MAANDOTHIYA

Contents

Acknowledgements

I would like to thank all the people who helped me accomplish this. And especially a friend who corrected all the mistakes in this book.

This is the first book of my life, and I have completed it in a long time, there may be room for some improvement in it, but due to paucity of time, I had to publish it now. I assure you not to give chance to complain next time.

Who I Am?

Am I quirky ..? Still I am Confused About myself.

I really love it... And something I aspire to be... Reflects me... Most powerful ways. I Am not immature but I have a deeper understanding just like we need fresh air to breathe. No day is really ever the same for me, and these days of my life are even more insane. Am not a backpacker, I'm not someone who up and quit his responsibility, abandoning his old lifestyle to the world without pause. I try not to sleep too late but also I'm not a morning person. It is exhausting, but I'm glad I do it as it may very well be my last.

I'm just A boy who managed to balance a career with my personal life, And I want to show you that you can do the same.

Sometimes I pretend to be funny and a lot of the time I find myself laughing at my own jokes. I am goofy and a child at heart. But, just because I am a child at heart doesn't mean I am immature and childish. There is a difference. I have an innocent personality but am not uneducated

CHAPTER ONE

WHAT ELSE DO YOU NEED TO KNOW ABOUT ME?

I'm kartik Mandothiya, Delhi is my birth town and little do we know it is bordered by the state of Haryana on three sides and by Uttar Pradesh to the east, For that reason, sometimes you will get a touch of the local language of Delhi as included little Bihari, Haryanvi or maybe Bhojpuri.

I'm a simple person who leverages technology to do my job. It's interesting how without a plan and without an idea you do your job not for passion but for the profession.
You just have a sound in your head that you do it once in your life and you actually do it not for your dreams but for your career and responsibility. By profession I am a VFX Artist also I am a VFX trainer but it's not my choice, and neither is my parent's. Actually, it can be just a coincidence or fate, which I am in this work. Little do we know, we're stronger than the tough phase of life, and also am not

getting my highest qualification. Sometimes everybody asks if it's good enough? But for me, it's not crazy yet.. because my dream has not come true.

To be honest, things aren't going all that well with the time with the flows and with the situations but somewhere the support of my family has always been huge for me with every major difficulty, and thankfully I never found myself standing alone where I need anyone.
Sometimes people ask me about my education because of my skills, but let me tell them that I do have not many highest qualifications. My past experience is not so good, in fact, I had failed in my college, so I couldn't start my studies. but now I am thinking to do it again. I want to learn more and yet I have learned a lot about it.

Honestly am getting bored of it and I want to learn something new. When I started I simply wanted to filmmaker but as you all know, situations and time required to do so, and since I was no stranger to programming and design, I leveraged those skills and start a journey of my profession, Now, I realized that I was able to make my dream come true. My dream is to become a film Maker. As we know, films are always inspiring us in different ways, and I need to Kickstart my career again so, so somewhere I want to this dream come true for me for the people who love and inspire me most. and my family also supports me in this, it is great that they are with me in this too.

I love fashion, movies, music, Designs, food, and even better Chai rather than Coffee. I believe to be different, as like nor two flowers of fragrance same. I m just a normal person as you everybody is, and my goal for this is to have a place where people can learn from my experience and mistakes while they grow up, just like fresh flowers blossom.

April 2019. Mumbai's first visit with my Father.

Basically, In the era of Badshah I fell in love with Kishore Kumar Ji songs I'm not old-fashioned but Arijit and Atif also remain constant in my music list. Just Because their songs always inspire me to make my dreams come true and to move forward.

> *"Ruk jana nahin tu kahin haar ke,*
> *Kaanton pe chalke, Milenge saaye bahaar ke."*
> *-Kishor Kumar*

So would you come along with me on this ride...?

Dream of mine..!

I have had many dreams in my childhood. I live my life pursuing my dreams and immersing myself in anything and everything that I love. I just have to travel everywhere, want to roam every moment and I have to work for it. Something for which no one can stop me to go anywhere.

You can't have regrets if you know that everything you did at the time was what you wanted but you sure can have regrets if you knew exactly what you wanted, yet chose to do nothing about it. Just as everyone starts thinking about their dreams, in the same way, I had already chosen some of my dreams for myself. And for one of them, I was inspired by a song from the movie Koi Mil Gaya which was like:-

"*En panchhiyo ko dekh kar jage hai yeh arman,
Dharatee pe ham chalte hai par chhulenge
aasman.*"

I had dreamed of becoming an astronaut at this same little age, not very good at studies, but as usual, it a dream that I had to fulfill, I had to roam not only in this world but in the whole universe. I love nature photography also.

November 2019. Diwali at Hawa Mahal Jaipur

Amer Mahal, Jaipur

Truth of every day...

A vision of transparency

There are so many things in life we can't explain.? Often times things happen for a reason and we are forced to deal with the outcome.? There are people I think about? every day who are no longer present in my life. Simply due to choices made by? themselves or an ongoing persuasion by? others. ?I have grown to accept reality and? move on.? Everybody knows how much I smile and keep my head up, but there is hurt and pain underneath because I remember it? always gets better. ?Somehow, some way.? I'm not perfect. ? I've also made mistakes.? ?

CHAPTER TWO

RANDOM THOUGHTS

Dear Tum...

Hey tum..!

Kya mene tumhe knhi dekha hai...knhi to dekha hoga yar... kisi bus me ya kisi CCD me.. Ya fir kisi yellow line ki last couch metro me, nahi nhi ye koi bahana nhi hai sach me ho skta hai

Kisi dost ki shaadi me ya kisi library me kya..! Tum books nhi padhti ho acha..!

But I am sure hum knhi to takraye hai kyuki tumhe dekh ke esa lagta hai mein tumhe janta to nhi pr phechanta jarur hu ho na ho par knhi to like dono kisi phn call pr honge ho samne se cross kiya ho, ya ho skta hai kisi bheed se excuse me khete hue nikle ho aur fir bheed me kho gye ho skata hai na.

Kanhi to dekha hoga hi hhhmmmm...... syd notice nhi kiya hoga. hum aksar kitne busy rhete h. insta pr apne latest update post krne me. ya kisi ko right person ko. tinder par left swipe krne me. Sirf unki DP dekh ke bina ye jane ki ye sirf pyar ke liye kafi nhi hai.

Kitna funny ha na ye hum sirf kuch ache filters ke piche apne aap ko ya apne bachpane ko chupane ki koshish krte hai just like me. Mere almost caption knhi na knhi se copied hote hai, nhi nhi esa nhi hai ki ye sab bhi sirf ek post hai copied hi sahi pr meri feelings bhi isse relate krti hai.

Umar kam pad jati hai..logo jaane me phechanne me or hum kuch seconds nhi lagate tinder ki ek profile se dusri me jaane me itne sare logo ko like unlike follow krne me hum bhool chuke hai ki ye pyar ka sahi proccess nhi hai hai na..!

Ab hum dono ko hi dekh lo kitne sare mouke the humare pas ek dusre se milne me ya jaane phechane me kash hum knhi milte or tumhara dupatta mere watch me atak jata how romatic na.

Ya knhi hum takra jate or tumhari books gir jati to syd books uthane me hi humara eye contact ho jata atleast 8 sec to hota hi , 8 sec kafi hai na love at first sight hone me sayad. Atleast mera ek bollywood sapna pura ho jata ho sakta tha ki mein tumhe is post me tag kr deta par hum dono hi busy the yar apne right person ko wrong place me dundhne me.

Itna jaldi me nhi yar fursat me pyar krna h mujhe blush krna hai mujhe bhi mere frnd bhi mujhe tumhare naam se preshan kr sakte the.
Tumhe dekh ke butterfly feel krni hai yar.
Wait.. 1 mint tumhe ye to nhi lg rha ki mein bhut chessy ho rha hu... ya freak out lag rha h tumhe nhi esa kuch bhi nhi.

acha hum agar fir knhi mile to yaad rkhna mein vhi hu jo sayad kisi metro ke last couch me tumhara wait krta ya kisi bus stand pr tuhara wait krta hua apne buse miss krta ya Counaght Place ki bheed ne ek jhlak dekh ke tumhara picha krta or fir knhi kho jata.

Things we do in love

You can spend a lot of your life waiting.

Waiting for your perfect partner, waiting for love, waiting for a new friendship, waiting for your turn, waiting to travel, waiting for some change, waiting until you feel ready to try something new, waiting for more time to do something...Waiting... Waiting... Waiting... It's empty spaces of time that you're waiting to live. I know I have fallen into this waiting phase. But you have got to get out yourself from this phase or you will look back and most likely regret that you did not live your life more.

Early Summer Days - 2020, Nahargarh Fort.

CHAPTER THREE

Unplanned Love Stories...!

Acceptance is the first step of any suffering. Accept that you are stuck with something and now you finally get over that suffering. That you're no longer part of someone's life. People can not love you as same as you love them and that's the reason breakups are the last solution to end the suffering inside you and you suffer from this pain for very long. The death of your happy relationship, and the memories you make and not able to recall everything again.

Sometimes I realized that love stories are not planned, they just happened, like an accident, or should I say just like the feeling where we stand in front of the ocean and slightly water touch are foot accidentally we know if we standing it's happened but sometimes inside we want this Because it's a most beautiful feeling ever. But mostly you want that you do not have to think about what is going on in our heart, but sometimes this kind of love just takes over you, somehow.

But love does not stop at just that, these many times this unconditional love always fulfills many conditions, such as the condition of changing yourself. The condition to make yourself like another. Where the first need is to love someone more than they love themselves, Where they want you to be like someone else, you live with them as their favorite people live with them. where no matter how much you trust them, they will be affected by how much you are jealous to see them with someone else. Jealousy, anger, possessiveness love, and these are also its qualities. But it is not that we want to assert our right over you, we are just afraid of losing our love. But no matter how much we try, we often do the same mistakes we avoid doing. Because of all these, we lose our most precious thing due to which we were together, our friendship.

And because of this one accident, we change everything despite not wanting to. Or maybe our destiny changes it.

But I personally believe that you need to keep up your efforts in your Love relationship to save that there is no love. But for the sake there is always one question in my mind "How was love if I had to live?" but now it all seems like breakups, Loveache, pain, Crying, and Giving its all are necessary to understand that what is life? It always brings a change. I remember Ranbir Kapoor's dialog "kabhi kabhi kanhi phunchne ke liye knhi se niklna jaruri hota hai." And I was ready for that change. or I waiting too..!!

CHAPTER FOUR

A Letter to Future Wife!

Hey, my dear future wife... Whenever you will be reading this letter, I do not know before you meet me or later. Do you know how I miss you every day? But I want to tell you something, why I am writing this letter to you. Are you probably the one whom my mother has liked for me? Well nowadays whenever we have a discussion about you in the house, I get lost in a dream. In your thoughts.
I can't think of anything other than you, just how we will be happy in the future?

I want to tell you something in this letter or I can say that I want to picturize some scenes of our future in this letter.

whenever my friends ask me about you, I always tell them that her eyes are the only Christmas lights that deserve to be seen all year long.

You should know some things about me before we are tied in 7 phere of Shaadi... Like I am not romantic but it is not that I do not know, I can convince you whenever you will be fought with me.
I can hold your hand in front of everyone.

Whenever I watch a movie or discover new songs, I start thinking about a hypothetical situation with you.

I want to roam at all my dream locations with you.

I am a bit emotional, therefore don't ever take undue advantage of me, I may get offended easily.?
you know what, I know how to cook, yes seriously ... but wait wait, that doesn't mean I'll always cook. No not at all...... but Yes, I will feed you with my hand.... I want to fulfill all your dreams as they would be my dreams also. I will love you with all your flaws. I will always be with you no matter what the moment. I will also stand by you in your tough times. I hope will meet at the right time and place.

Till then take care.? I will miss you.
And thank you for my future better half.

With love...
Your future husband... ☺

CHAPTER FIVE

TO MY WIFE

Maybe I'm too late to be your first but right now I am preparing myself to be your last. My life has been a rollercoaster ride with a lot many ups and downs. I never knew what being happy felt like until you walked into my life.

You not only were there when I needed you but are someone who understands my silence too maybe... You are like that white color of my life who just made my life peaceful and soothing by just existing in my life.

The first meeting with any person is special and if that person is the one whom you have chosen as a partner for the journey of your life then that meeting becomes even more special.

Our life together will be wonderful, of that I am sure. but I also realize that we'll have some ups and downs in this relationship. It won't be a smooth sail always... but with the two of us together, every ride will be one to remember.

and don't you worry baby, because even though I may look all sweet and dainty, I will stand next to you like a rock if you ever need me. yes, we'll have our fights, our little differences but that's what relationships are about right?

If you would feel angry, just scream at me, I won't say a single word, if you feel love, just express it. I will hug you. In other words, just express yourself. we will become best friends. we will tease each other. we will go for a long walk together after a hectic schedule. if the time ever comes when you realize you would be happier without me than with me please tell me. your happiness is an integral part of my own, and I want what's best for you even if that is no longer me. this is the only way I know how to love.

CHAPTER SIX

HEY DEAR, INSPIRATION..!

Hey dear, Inspiration....or should I say you duffer, Because sometimes you just behave like that. ok, leave....!

How are you Maybe your answer will be as usual, happy. I am not so good at writing and you also know that. I talk very little, and I cannot write what I feel. But still, I am writing for you, a letter.

When I first saw you, or we met, it was our first meeting. But perhaps we had gone through it many times before. You used to tell me like this.

When I saw you for the first time, When you wore a jacket with rollover sleeves, with Tying hair, when you came into class, Then I saw you for the first time. On winter days. By the way, I have heard one thing many times That we often meet or separate someone on winter days only.

We often need friends with whom we can share everything. And you are one of them, and I do not even share this much with my GF. I can tell you anything that I want to say. I know you will never be bored. Whether it is a love story of mine or my own story when I was born in 1996. Do you Remember that night... ye kahani tab ki hai jab mein hua tha.... HAHAHAAA..!

You know what, You are alike the dream of everyone, maybe mine also. Whenever I think about you, often only one song comes to my mind – Ha tum bilkul vesi ho... Jesa mene Socha Tha....!. I sometimes wonder what you try to hide. Is your smile true or does it even try to hide anything? What is that that hurts you? How can someone be so happy? I know you probably won't answer me. But I want to tell you something, stay the same as you always are. I am happy that you teach me and explain, what to do or not. But every time it is better to take care of yourself rather than solve the problem of others. You need it. This world is a little selfish and you should understand it. Yes, I know you are very intelligent from childhood, but still.

And you please stop knowing my weakness. Now you already know more about me more than me. One day, you will read this but please Don't laugh at me. Just remember that moment when we used to talk a lot late at night, About the moon. You are a little crazy. You talk to the fruit, how mad you are. And you talk too much. But I like to listen to you, I can always argue with you no matter what the topic is. Remember this moment. What I might have been thinking or feeling. Thinking about it now made me laugh a bit. And smile.

This is already too long. I hope you're smiling too. And maybe laughing a bit. Coz I am being silly. Which is rare for me. I cannot promise that I will continue to write more thoughts. But I want to. Because you taught me this. I want to write what I feel, what I think.

CHAPTER SEVEN

A LETTER TO FRIEND, WHOM I CARED..!

Dear Friend.....

Do you remember our first date, that first date of tea, yes I am talking about it. Was it very good na? Of course, you will remember, What great days those were. *Mano Kal ki hi baat hai.*

And remember that day when I fought with my mother and left home. How much I cried in front of you. You know I cried in front of you for the first time. And you were the one who wiped my tears

You've been there through all of my ups and downs. You've been there when I needed support. You were there to scream at me when I made stupid mistakes.

Please never change who you are because you are seriously perfect for me or for my friendship. I will always be there to wipe your tears.

Today I was listening to that song *"Tera yaar hu main"* and suddenly guess what, I felt like I needed to talk to you and I want to share many things which were happening in my life. It wasn't that anything was wrong or that anything had happened, it was just a moment where things suddenly weren't good for a few minutes between us. Ahhhh....! Don't worry These moments are random as you know my mood swings hahaaaa.....

Life has a not-so-great way of reminding us that a lot of things are possible and the best we can do is make sure we can keep going. It's not possible to be prepared or to fix every situation, so take a deep breath and remember that it's okay to cry. But remember that this time you will not be able to cry on my shoulder.

You always used to complain to me that I never talk to you or I ever share anything, So here are some things that I never told you.

You were the first girl whom I dated.

You were the first girl with whom I loafed.

You were the one who roam on my scooty for hours with me and the first girl with whom I took a tour of the scooter.

If you were to ask me now where I think we stand, I would say we're just friends now. But if you asked me that time, I would say that We were more than friends. We are way past just friends and you know it. We aren't together, though, and I am completely fine with that, I really am.

But overall, I promise I will be there to keep making amazing memories till the end of time.?

> *"Tu jo rootha toh kaun hansega, Tu jo chhuta toh kaun rahega !*
> *Tu chup hai toh yeh darr lagta hai, Apna mujhko ko ab kaun kahega !"*

CHAPTER EIGHT

DEAR BEST FRIEND, I WISH I COULD TELL YOU HOW I FEEL

That time when you told me to express my secret feelings to you .... *or tumne ye bhi kha ki dil ki bate bol deni chahiye... jesa ki Apne Kha tha ki aapko express feeling jyada achi lagti h...* I thought you finally knew. *Mujhe laga ki tum samjhti ho mujhe ya mere Pyar ko..* but then you told me you want to say that to someone else. It broke my heart. no, it broke me. unfortunately, we've always been like this – me being madly in love with you, and you choosing someone else who will break your heart in the end.

you'd confide in me and I'd think about telling you how I feel, but I never could. perhaps, I didn't want to lose you as a friend.

my feelings got worse at night. how many times I have promised myself to stop loving you – to give up on you and me. I'd tell myself to text less and slowly fade away, but whenever you'd text, I'd just give in.

I have tried distancing myself from you, but I failed. all you'd do is send me a insta reels or just look at me and smile and I'll be head over heels in love with you.

I have been trying to not write about you, but this process is catharsis – it eases my feelings. and then, my writings are all we talk about – if I gave it up, you just might stop talking to me.

I often wonder if you know how I feel, but I don't say anything because you say you're afraid to lose me, too. you like what you have between us.

*Par mujhe kabhi kabhi esa lagta h ki tum janti ho ki mein kya feel krta hu ..par tum fir bhi sab chupaye rakhne ki sajish krti ho...*you're just hinting to not confess because you don't feel the same way... *esa hi h na....*

I wish I could tell you how I feel, but how can I do something that just might make you sad? after all, what is love if not seeing the one you love being happy?

To My Dearest Friend

Hey dost ..hws u..??
Well, I want to thank u,.. thank u for being in my life,
thank u for some boring lectures, for some advice some
life-changing advice... and some financial advice also...
Thank u for giving me the strength to fight my own mood
swings or my own battle...

Kabhi kabhi mein sochta hu ki hum sholay ke JAY or
VEERU na hoke... kuch kuch hota hai ke.. Rahul or Anjali
hote to...but... BTW
specially thank u for being *JAY* of this VEERU...
U know what I can't wait for both of us to get older and
tell our kids about all the crazy shits which we've done
together...
Or apne liye upar ek special bartan me teil garam ho rha h...
jaldi aaiyo...pakode banege..humare....kyuki ache karam to
kiye ni honge... h na...

"Aaj agar bhar aai hain, Boondein baras jaayengi
Kal kya pata kinn ke liye aankhein taras
jaayengi."

CHAPTER NINE

UNSAID EMOTIONS

Phir Suna Meethi Meethi Si Woh Dastaan...

The rain often gives us many memories, some memories from which we might never want to go away. One evening of such rain when I was going home from the office. The rain was very heavy, so traffic and autos were not working a lot, so after waiting a long time, I had to book a cab. The distance was not long but today it was very late and to pass this time radio was running in the car but my focus was more on the drops of rain than the songs that were touching my hand. She often enjoyed the rain like this.
Then suddenly a song played on the radio and my memories deepened with that song.

> "*Phir suna meethi meethi si woh dastaan*
> *Jisko sunke meri zindagi me hoti hai nayi subah*
> *Pass aa, aake mujhse phir na door jaa*
> *Pyari pyari iss raat ki geharaaiyon mein doob ja*
> *Wo oo.. wo oo.. wo oo.. oo..*"

Sometimes a moment gets stuck in a song and in this song I was stuck with Sashi. Or should I say that when I told her that I love you and she said that I love you too but after some time, she said that she loves Dhruv and I said that I still love you. But she didn't mind, and me, as always. whenever I hear this song or when I see that movie ticket in my bag when we watched the movie together.

Someone told me that I am broken, And My all the broken pieces fix it as they needed or just for temporary happiness .. so I am dissipated every time .. like I was dissipated once again ... when I saw her again... ..not in front of me but on my Insta account. ..

I was scrolling my insta as usual and suddenly my fingers stopped when I saw the picture of her ... When I read her name to confirm it was the same but a little confused... My heart beats faster but not like before but the butterflies in my stomach not flying this time that pin of sensation in my body is quite different and my hands still shaking... And all those days were back in front of my eyes .. which we had spent together ..It had been 5 years but I still had not forgotten all that.

We cannot force anyone to stay in our life... And we cannot stop anyone who wants to go... This life is a journey and We only have a responsibility to complete this... Yes, We often make relationships in this journey ... but we have to accept that she too has her own journey ... which she has to complete in her own way ... and What we call a heartbreak is just a break... Just like stop at the Tapri on the way, a break of chai and biscuits... and think that it is good for you to sit there and remember the same old journey. Or have to go ahead ... For new memories in a new journey ...

Everyone comes into your life for some reason ... Because without meaning we don't even give time to ourselves ...
par har bar kagjo par dard ki numaish krne se acha hai ki mein sab bhul jau... par ek din mei realise krta hu ki agr mein kosish kru tuti hui chijo ko vps jodne ki to mei humesha fail ho jata hu kyu ki bikhri hui chijo ko sameta ja ja sakta hai par tuti hui chijo ko nhi...becos that is what I am now. But This time I scrolled up without leaving heart on her pics...:)

CHAPTER TEN

A Friend I Got Used To

Kitni preshan hoti hongi ye ungliya bhi jo ye janti h ki samne wala inse preshan ho jayega fr bhi kr deti h ye msg bina soche samjhe..

Hum sab apni apni life me busy hote hai .... sabke pas itna time nhi h ki ek dusre ke liye waqt nikala jaye ya syd waqt bhi km h jo hum har kisi ko de bhi nhi sakte

Agr koi tumhe msg kr rha h puch rha h fikr krta h tumhari to uske liye to tumhe waqt dena jaruri hua na

Thik hai tumhari life me bhi kuch log ese honge jinko tumhe waqt dena jaruri lgta h

Lakin agr koi tumse pyar kre... or use jahir krne k liye tumhara waqt mange .. to syd tumhari life me uski jarurt utni nhi hogi

Lakin uske liye to ho skta h ki syd tumhi sabse jyada jaruri ho

Kisi se attach ho jana bhut aasan h or ajib h

Khud se hum kisi ko feel nhi krwa sakte h.. Or samne wala khud se feel krle ye bhut kam chance me hota hai

Manta hu ki Jyada msg krna jyada possesive ho jana glt h

Lakin usko kya mtlb sahi glt se .. jisko sirf tumse bat krne se mtlb h vo syd nhi samjhta hoga ki itna bhi koi bsy rheta h apni life me... ho skta h vo sirf tumhe khone se drta h kyuki uske liye tum sabse jyada jaruri ho...

Uska jyadatar waqt sirf tumhare liye hota hoga vo bekhbar is bat se ki usko tumhare waqt ki jarurt kya h..

Pyar pgl kr deta h jisme samjhne jesa kuch nhi bachata h...kyuki iski jarurt esi hoti h..jinke liye manjil to h pr tumhare liye koi rasta nhi h

Waqt lagega samjhne or samjhane me khud ko

Waqt lagega haqiqt bnane me isko ..fr syd tumhare liye ye ungliyan itna pareshan nhi hogi ya tumhe preshan nhi krengi

rishta tabhi strong hota hai jab uski neev strong ho iskeliye waqt dena jaruri ha

Waqt tumhara bhi jaruri h ...or waqt mera bhi jaruri h ...

Frk itna h mera tumhare liye jaruri h...

Or tumhara ..syd ...syd nhi ...

Kitni preshan hoti hongi ye ungliya bhi........!

CHAPTER ELEVEN

MY UNINVITED MOOD SWINGS

We all have been there. the last time when you wanted to talk to someone and you reached till the end of your contact list and didn't find a name? that time I really need a friend.

Has it ever happened to you that a strange feeling comes to mind? A sentiment that has no name or is probably in a dictionary of science? You are doing something very important, then suddenly a strange peace and you stop there. You start feeling very sad and lonely in a moment. Where does this feeling come from?

Like you are talking with someone, then suddenly only a sound is heard in your ears, but you do not understand what they are saying.
It is like someone unplugged your "happy fuse". you no longer feel the way you were feeling moments ago.

then there are days when you don't even need anyone. you sit down with a cup of chai and you play some nice music. in those moments, it feels a little less lonely. but then the song ends, or you finish your cup of chai. and then loneliness comes knocking on your door like an uninvited guest. it sits down on your couch and refuses to leave your room until the next morning.

This happened often to me, I often calm down suddenly but don't know why. I want to cry but there are no tears in my eyes. I lose something in my head, I also want to tell everyone, but they don't understand why this is so and then due to this also my relationship gets spoiled many times, no one understands this And I can't explain to them that this is my uninvited mood swings. And what is the reason why I do not even know?

Is it always necessary to be such a chill bro type? no cannot always be like this.
kyuki mujhse nhi ho pata , mujhe fark padta hai.
Yes, I know that for many people it is a very useless or unnecessary thing, but I am not that kind of person. I need a person with whom I can share everything, which I have not told anyone to till date, my all untold stories. We try to always be positive or to be chill.

"Khaali hath shaam Aayi hai, Khaali hath jaayegi,
Aaj bhi na aaya koi, Khaali lout Jayegi...!"

CHAPTER TWELVE

SHORT STORY

Mein humesa ki trha office se niklta or jb mann krta to to samne hi mall me chala jata ...mano ye mera daily ka rutin ho gya...agr kisi din hajri nhi lgayi to to salry me peise to nhi bt kuch tha esa jo mein miss krne se drta tha....aaj bhi mein humesa ki trha apni duty puri kr rha tha....aaj 24 april tha vo din jb mein pheli baar disha se mila tha...vhi disha jisme meri syd hr samsya ki rah mil jaya krti thi...mrea pyar...

aaj hume 1 saal ho gya tha .....

are dost kese ho....khana khaya ya nhi...

nhi...abhi koi khilane wala nhi ...mene turnt hi bol diya tha...

to uska jwab mjak me hi shi bt hum dono ko ek krne me vhi jimmedar tha...

usne kha to thodi si shaadi krle mujhse....

.... ye iteffaq tha ya kuch or pta nhi....mein usse kai dino se esi hi kuch baat bolna chahta tha ....pr kbhi himmt hi nhi hui......

kuch dino baad to mano mere aas pass wala koi anjan vyakti bhi mujhe mera rishtedaar lagta tha...aata jata mein kisi ke bhi haal chaal puch liya krta tha......aakhir nya nya pyar jo hua tha...

jb hum dino akser mila krte to thodi si shaadi ki icha ho jati ...ek din mein usseke sath radha krishna mandir chla

gya...or vhi ....uske sath pure 4 fere le liye the...baaki 3 usne mujhpr udhar chod diye....boli ki byaj ke sath vapas legi....
aaj hi ka vo din tha .....
aaj mujhpr vo baaki k 3 fere ek bojh se bante ja rhe the.....
pta nhi vo q isse bhul gyi thi...

mein yhi soch kr aaj bhi beitha rheta tha...
tabhi achanak mera phn baja...
hello.....
hello kartik ....
ye awaz ....mein syd ise kbhi bhul nhi skta tha....
ye disha ki hi aawaz thi....
mene bhi ese hi use ignor krna chahta tha aakhir mein bhi gussa tha...use phele hi man jana chahiye to bhut baar sry bhi bola tha..pr kambakht dil hi nhi man rha tha....
or phn utha hi liya...
mujhe tumse kl milna......
usne itna hi kha tha...or phn cut kr diya...
kb or khan ye to btaaya hi nhi ...
pr syd mujhe pta tha....vhi radha krishna mandir ...hum akservhi mila krte the...
to ab tym to mujhe pta nhi tha...pr mein to subha subha ghr se 8 bje ese bhaga jese late ho jane pr nokri jane ka drr ho....aakhir mein usse khona nhi chahta tha.....
8...se 10...fir....2.....fir dekhte dekhte ....shaam ka 7 bje gye....or mene aasman me dekha to mano sare taare mujhpr hans rhe ho.....mein subha se uska intjar kr rha tha...uske liye gift bhi laya tha...

ab aakir hadd hoti h yar....
aaj koi april fool ka day to tha nhi...tabhi mujhe piche se ek aawaz sunai di...ye disha to nhi pr uska khat aaya to jo uski dost lekr aayi thi....
whatsapp or fb jese tym me khat ....ye ajib nhi tha ....jab bhi esi koi baat hoti thi jo hum khe nhi pate the...akser khat likh

kr diya krte...

jb mene usse padhna shuru kiya....to mere chere pr se use dekhne ki meri aasha ....mano dheere dhhere ja rhi ho....

kartik mujhe pta h syd tum mera intjar bhut tym se ki rhe ho...par ab mein tumse kabhi milna hi nhi chah rhi thi....actuall me meri shaadi tay ho gyi h...uska naam sunil h ....yhi delhi me rheta h...ache ghr se h....hum dono kai dino se jante h ek dusre ko....humari dosti achi hui to ghr walo ne bhikoi aaptti nhi jtai...

mein is khat me bs tumse judi ek chij lota rhi hu....

ye Ring ....

ye vhi ring thi jo mene use ek auto me sabke sath hote hue..bhi bina kisi ko dikhaye sabse najre churate hue usse phenai thi....

ek tym tha jb vo kabhi ise nikalti bhi nhi thi...or aaj...

ye khat khatm hua hi tha ....jb uski dost ne mere hath me uski ring pakda di.....

or mere hath me jo ek bda sa box tha ...jo gift ke tor par mein disha ka dene ke liye laya tha,...mere hath se gir gya....

mene ring usse li ...or piche ki chlne lga....aasman se aaj bin mousam barsat hui thi....jo mere aansu ko chupane ki kosish kr rhi ...

uski vo saheli .... ne jb vo gift ka box dekha tha .jisme kuch khat the to jo mene disha ko dene ke liye likhe jarur the par kabhi use de nhi paya tha....ek trofi thi jo disha ne mujhe di thi...jb vo first tym singing compition me jeet kr llayi thi or mujhe di...thi...ek khat tha jisse uski dost padhne ki kosish to kr rhi thi....bt barsat ki choti choti bund usse ink ko bhiga rhi thi...or use padhne se rok rhi thi,,......

9 7 9 8 8 8 7 1 7 5 8 9 8